The Enormous Turnip

Retold by Katie Daynes

Illustrated by Georgien Overwater

One rosy pink morning
a farmer whistled his way to work.

It was time to pick some turnips.

You'll do nicely!

The farmer grabbed the turnip's leaves in both hands and heaved with all his might.

The turnip didn't budge.

"I'd better give him a hand,"
said the farmer's wife.

She hugged the farmer,
  he grabbed the turnip
    and they both tugged and tugged...

...but the turnip
didn't budge.

Jack was watching from an apple tree.
"Come and help," called his father.

Jack dashed across the field.
He took hold of his mother's skirt.

His mother hugged the farmer,
the farmer grabbed the turnip
and they all tugged and tugged...

...but the turnip
didn't budge.

"Woof!" barked the farmer's dog.
The dog yanked Jack's shirt.

Jack gripped his mother's skirt.

She hugged the farmer.

He grabbed the turnip and everybody **heaved**.

Still the turnip didn't budge.

All of a sudden, a cat bit the dog's tail.

The dog ripped Jack's shirt.

Jack tore his mother's skirt.

She let go of the farmer...

...and they all tumbled
to the ground.

"We'll try one last time," sighed the farmer.
Just then, a little robin flew by.

The robin pecked the cat's tail,

the cat bit the dog's tail,

the dog yanked Jack's shirt,

Jack gripped his mother's skirt,

she hugged the farmer,

he grabbed the turnip...

...and everybody heaved.

Slowly, very slowly,

the turnip began to move.

It's big.

It's huge.

It's enormous!

Woof!

Meow!

Tweet!

At long last, as the sun slipped out of sight,
the turnip POPPED out of the ground.

Everyone slept well that night.

The following day, Jack and his
mother chopped up the turnip.

They had turnip soup for lunch...

turnip soup for supper...

and turnip soup
for breakfast...

Turnip

Turnip Jam

...every day for a month.

Next year I'm growing carrots!

About the story

The Enormous Turnip is a Russian folk tale.
Some versions have a little mouse helping
out at the end, instead of a bird.

Edited by Lesley Sims
Designed by Sam Whibley

First published in 2014 by Usborne Publishing Ltd., Usborne House, 83-85 Saffron Hill,
London EC1N 8RT, England. www.usborne.com Copyright © 2014 Usborne Publishing Ltd.